# MARCIA VAUGHAN

### Illustrated by *Ann Schweninger*

# We're Going on a Ghost Hunt

SCHOLASTIC INC.

New York  Toronto  London  Auckland  Sydney
Mexico City  New Delhi  Hong Kong  Buenos Aires

D1294703

*For Rosemary Stimola, one sharp cookie!*
—M. V.

*For Maggie Byer-Sprinzeles*
—A. S.

ISBN 0-439-44523-X

12 11 10 9 8 7 6 5 4 3 2 1               2 3 4 5 6 7/0

Printed in the U.S.A.                24

First Scholastic printing, October 2002

The illustrations in this book were created in linoleum cut, then printed with
oil base block-printing ink and enhanced with watercolor paint.

The display type was set in Bernhard Antique.
The text type was set in Minion Semibold.

Designed by Linda Lockowitz

Do you want to go on a ghost hunt
to catch a trick-or-treat ghost?
We're not afraid.
No, we're not afraid.
No, we're not afraid at all!

Looking high.
Looking low.
Off on a ghost hunt.
Here we go!

Oh, dear. What have we here?
A swamp.
An *ooky spooky* swamp.
What will we do?
We'll wade across!
*Romp* and *stomp.*
*Romp* and *stomp.*
Across the *ooky spooky* swamp.

We're going on a ghost hunt
to catch a trick-or-treat ghost.
We're not afraid.
No, we're not afraid.
No, we're not afraid at all!

Looking high.
Looking low.
Off on a ghost hunt.
Here we go!

Oh, dear. What have we here?
A haunted house.
A haunted house,
where goblins go thump.
What will we do?
We'll dash past.
*Rumpety bump.*
*Rumpety bump.*
Past a haunted house,
where goblins go thump.

We're going on a ghost hunt
to catch a trick-or-treat ghost.
We're not afraid.
No, we're not afraid.
No, we're not afraid at all!

Looking high.
Looking low.
Off on a ghost hunt.
Here we go!

Oh, dear. What have we here?
Bats.
Big black bats, all furry and fat.
What will we do?
We'll *scurry*
under.
*Skitter* and *scat*.
*Skitter* and *scat*.
Under big black bats,
all furry and fat.

We're going on a ghost hunt
to catch a trick-or-treat ghost.
We're not afraid.
No, we're not afraid.
No, we're not afraid at all!

Looking high.
Looking low.
Off on a ghost hunt.
Here we go!

Oh, dear. What have we here?
Skeleton bones.
Skeleton bones that dance about.
What will we do?
We'll fly by.
*Run* and *shout.*
*Run* and *shout.*
By skeleton bones that dance about.

We're going on a ghost hunt
to catch a trick-or-treat ghost.
We're not afraid.
No, we're not afraid.
No, we're not afraid at all!

Looking high.
Looking low.
Off on a ghost hunt.
Here we go!

Oh, dear. What have we here?
A cave.
A creepy cave,
where the old ghost dwells!
What will we do?
We'll crawl through.
*Oh…so…slow.*
*Oh…so…slow.*
Into the creepy cave we go.

"Uh-oh. Do you see what *I* see?"
"Is it a rock?"
"Does a rock have long arms?"
"Is it a bush?"
"Does a bush have a *twirling, swirling* body?"
"Is it a mossy log?"
"Does a mossy log have *big round* eyes?"
"I give up. What do you see?"

"A ghost.
A great big scary ghost!
Off we go!"

Oh so *slow.* Oh so *slow.*
Out of the creepy cave we *go....*

*Run* and *shout*. *Run* and *shout*.
By skeleton bones
that dance about…

*Skitter* and *scat*. *Skitter* and *scat*.
Under big black bats,
all furry and fat . . .

*Rumpety bump. Rumpety bump.*
Past the haunted house,
where goblins go thump . . .

*Romp* and *stomp. Romp* and *stomp.*
Across the *ooky spooky* swamp ...

Hurry. Hurry.
*Fast, fast, fast.*
Slam the door.
Safe—at last.

"I was looking for you!"

"We went on a ghost hunt
to catch a trick-or-treat ghost.
We weren't afraid.
No, we weren't afraid.
No, we weren't afraid at all!"